No Chocolate

Written and Illustrated by Julie House

Dedicated to Sammy House

Once in a lifetime
Never find another like him
In a thousand years

Sammy the dachshund
Loved each new day
"Tug of war", "Chase your tail"
Were fun games he would play

He loved sunshine and scratches
This floppy-eared dude
But his favorite thing of all things
Was good FOOD

But we're not talking dog food
No, not good enough
Real HUMAN food
Was the flavorful stuff

From Salmon to hot dogs
From Carrots to cheese
If it was food meant for PEOPLE
Sam was not hard to please

His master would spoil him
This made Sammy proud
But one tasty treat
Sam was never allowed

"You CANNOT have chocolate"
His master would say
"It's not good for dogs Sam,
So remember, OK?"

But how could something
Like CHOCOLATE be bad?
It seemed like the ultimate
Treat humans had

It made Sam's mouth water
when he got just one whiff
It smelled like the yummiest scent
He could sniff

One day as Sam lay
In the summertime sun
His master came home
From a big grocery run

Bringing bag after bag
To the house from outside
Scents were filling the air
Sam's mouth hung open wide

He caught wind of some sausage
Then turkey and ham
Bleu cheese, tuna salad
All favorites for Sam

But one luscious scent
Stood out from the rest
Sweet, smooth tempting chocolate
Smelled the absolute BEST

As his master continued
To put food away
He was holding the chocolate
When Sam heard him say

"No chocolate for Sammy"
He looked Sam in the eye
"It's not good for doggies"
But Sam wondered why

Taking the bag
His master opened it wide
Into a dish
Clinked the candy inside

He carried the dish
To his desk in a flash
Sam watched him hide it
In his drawer's secret stash

His master caught glimpse of
Sam's interested stare
So he turned back to Sammy
And repeated with care

"No chocolate for Sammy
Now Sam, I must go
The lawn is lengthy again
I must mow

I'll be back when I'm done
In an hour or more
And we'll play in the yard
You can wait by the door"

Sam waited and watched
For a minute or four
Until his mind wandered
To the treats in the drawer

"Just one glimpse of chocolate
Is all that I need
I'll just glance, take a peek"
Such a small harmless deed

So into the office
Sam quietly sneaked
He opened the drawer
In the desk with a creak

Up wafted the smell
That had called him for years
He looked at the candy
And trembled with fear

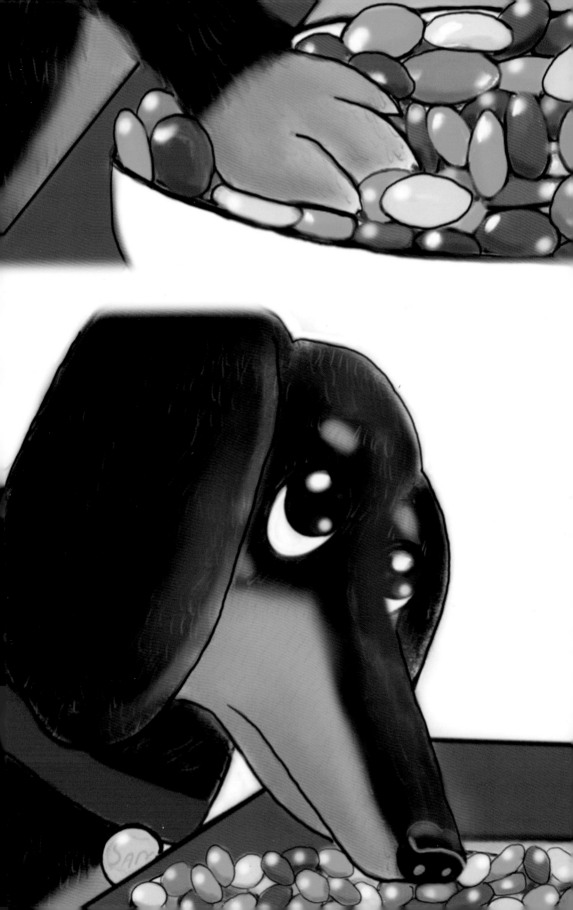

"I'll just feel the chocolate"
Oh he craved it so much
His paw stroked the candy
It felt smooth to the touch

"I'll just SMELL the chocolate
Then I'll be content"
He sniffed and inhaled
The magnificent scent

The looking and touching
And sniffing brought doubt
At least one of his senses
Felt completely left out

"Chocolate couldn't be bad"
He concluded in haste
"And to know it for certain
I just need one TASTE"

"Just one taste of a chocolate
Couldn't be a big deal"
Thought Sammy just as
The temptation got real

He stuck out his tongue
For the smallest of licks
And one piece went missing
Like a great magic trick

Then one piece turned to two
And two turned to four
Sam was out of control
And he kept eating more

That chocolate was feeding
His tongue and His soul
Until he looked down
At the big empty bowl

"Oh what have I done"
Sammy cried real dog tears
He stopped wagging his tail
And he lowered his ears

He was feeling ashamed
And was scared what would come
When his master returned
And the chocolate was gone

The lawnmower stopped
"I must hide, but oh, where?"
He wondered and whined
& ran behind the blue chair

He heard the door open
Heard his kind master say
"Oh Sammy, where are you?
Are you ready to play?"

But Sam did not feel like playing
Not one little bit
For his tummy was rumbling
And he was gonna be sick

He came out from hiding
That miserable pup
And all of the chocolate he downed
Came back up

"Oh no" cried his master
Who ran over to help
As Sam threw up more
By the door with a yelp

His master seemed saddened
He was tender and sweet
"Come here little buddy
Now just what did you eat?"

As the master looked closely
He realized the problem
"The CHOCOLATE? Oh, Sammy!"
His master was solemn

"This was just why I warned you
To keep far away
I didn't want you sick Sam,
Finding out the hard way!"

The master hugged sorry Sam
And he cleaned up his mess
And Sam realized his master
Always knew best

Sam understood he
Was a true, faithful friend
And Sammy could trust him
From now 'til the end

Furables

...fables & fun for your little one

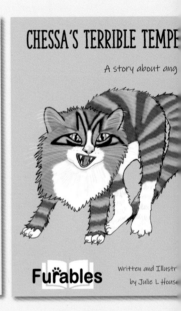

Book #1 a story about fear

Book #2 a story about temptation

Book #3 a story about anger

Find Furables at littleoneshop.com!

little one shop

NO CHOCOLOATE FOR SAMMY

1st Printing 2020

Furables Book #2

ISBN 978-164871095-7

Copyright © 2020 by Julie House